A Room For Sorrow:
Five Short Stories

A Room For Sorrow: Five Short Stories

Dorothy M. Hong

iUniverse, Inc.
New York   Bloomington

A Room For Sorrow: Five Short Stories

iUniverse books may be ordered through booksellers or by contacting:

iUniverse
1663 Liberty Drive
Bloomington, IN 47403
www.iuniverse.com
1-800-Authors (1-800-288-4677)

Because of the dynamic nature of the Internet, any Web addresses or links contained in this book may have changed since publication and may no longer be valid. The views expressed in this work are solely those of the author and do not necessarily reflect the views of the publisher, and the publisher hereby disclaims any responsibility for them.

ISBN: 978-1-4401-5380-8 (pbk)
ISBN: 978-1-4401-5381-5 (ebk)

Printed in the United States of America

iUniverse rev. date: 7/23/2009

Table of Contents

PREFACE

"The eye of man hath not heard, the ear of man hath not seen, man's hand is not able to taste, his tongue to conceive, nor his heart to report, what my dream was." Act IV, Scene I of Shakespeare's <u>A Midsummer Night's Dream</u>

People generally write to shed truth from knowledge, to restore human dignity from ridicule and for pleasure. Publication serves to share information and to express freedom from becoming prisoners of stupidity, greed and power and gives enormous catharsis to both reader and writer thereby giving tools with which one can act or refrain from certain conducts as a result of knowledge.

To me, pursuit of happiness from having made personal decisions from free will as oppose to "devil made me do it,' or "my body is my destiny" arguments appropriately allocates a set of responsibilities to the society in which one lives. Lives of immigrants of color from other continents remain largely unexamined in the mainstream America so I offer these stories to have a glimpse of peculiar set of issues confronting young Korean American women in particular and humanity in general pointing to ultimate depravity of mankind if left unchecked.

I give thanks to iUniverse, Interdisciplinary Nineteenth-Century Studies Conference (April, 2009) and Friedrich Schiller (1759-1805) in shaping my mind to write and publish this book.

The original inhabitants of present Korean peninsula were Aryan nomads who settled there via the Eurasia Steppe traversing Russia and China into Korea. Before their arrival were aborigines on the dry land. Since then there had been mass migration of Chinese and invasions by Mongolians, French and Japanese.

As the descendant of Yangban during Yi dynasty who paid tribute as emissary at one time to Chinese emperor of bygone days, of clan who were chief warriors who helped found Yi dynasty, then fought against the French in 1866 and finally resisted against the Japanese Occupation in 1919, it is not surprising that after the Korean War of 1950 and subsequent to Civil Rights Movement in the seventies that my family immigrated to this nation of blessed wonders of diversity of population, abundance of commodities and wide gamut bordering extremities of ideas and associations out of which Korean immigrants appreciate work ethics, frugality, proper rest and worship.

Koreans come from long tradition of considering their hair and outer coating from parents as one of the most revered assets and so they have an obligation to take good care. This tradition provides a rich platform for free speech juxtaposing one's innate need to reach outward to feel like a whole person in a community while preserving the legacy from one's parents.

I realize that my free speech will undoubtedly leave room for discord but as my pastor sent me a passage to read in the bible during my personal crisis I relay this passage here for the morale and health:

"Rejoice in the Lord always; again I will say, Rejoice. Let all men know your forbearance. The Lord is at hand. Have no anxiety about anything, but in everything by prayer and supplication with thanksgiving let your request be made known to God. And the peace of God, which passes all understanding, will keep your hearts and your minds in Christ Jesus." ---Philippians 4:4-7---

Dorothy M. Hong

Bronxville, New York

June 2009

Dorothy M. Hong

<u>A Well Meant Chance Meeting</u> is a short story revolving around Jenna Hong and her two buddies in her sorority at an Ivy League school.

The story offers a realistic glimpse of three Korean American young women from similar immigrant backgrounds making the most of their situations in an integrated American society against the expectations of the model minority myth and their parents' vicariously living through their children's seemingly envious social experiences. In the end, even a failure is the mother of success story and one success story deserves another.

A WELL MEANT CHANCE MEETING
BY DOROTHY HONG
(FICTION)

After the induction ceremony at Alpha Phi, Mary, Jenna and Linda by accident shared a same table at a local restaurant along with other members of the same sorority to celebrate their new sisterly bond as active members together. At first Mary, Jenna and Linda felt awkward sitting together as they were the only three Asian members of Alpha Phi and at first brush their sitting together looked like self-imposed segregation.

They talked about their hometowns, their hobbies, their intended majors and their career aspirations. Mary Yoon comes from Rockville, Maryland while Jenna Hong comes from Brooklyn, New York and Linda Lee comes from Miami, Florida. Mary spoke avidly about running while Jenna shared her mugging experience in a New York City subway station. Linda was waiting her turn

and thinking quietly forming in her mind words she was going to use to describe her ambition of becoming a trial lawyer. Mary was athletic and seemed a bit butchy but Jenna's and Linda's suspicion of Mary being a possible lesbian was allayed when they learned that Mary had a boyfriend. Jenna has unusually black hair, so black that they look blue and silvery. It was a rare occasion that Jenna spoke up. She usually keeps things to herself and rarely speaks her mind. But Jenna felt an instant bond with Mary and Linda and felt that she could trust them with her private affairs.

"Did the police apprehend your mugger?" asked Linda.

Jenna shook her head. "It was better that the mugger snatched my purse and ran away than for me to chase him and irk him even more," Jenna summed up.

Mary and Linda became quiet momentarily.

Linda spoke knowledgeably about becoming a lawyer.

"I know in the past in Korea, women lawyers were either unmarriageable or they ended up becoming Suzy homemaker. But that's because Korea is not a litigious society so there aren't very many lawyers like here in America. So lawyers occupy much more prestigious social position in Korea, unlike here. I think everyone needs a lawyer at some point in life in America. And I want to be useful in that way," Linda said quietly.

She wanted so much to be a lawyer and this was the first time she was able to articulate her desire. Her lips trembled a little bit as she articulated these words.

Mary forewarned Linda, "As a lawyer in America you can become phenomenally rich and famous. On the other hand, you can become depressed and stay poor the rest of your life. My next-door neighbor told me. He is a lawyer."

Then Jenna asked looking at Mary and Linda, "Are you both Korean?"

They both nodded. Jenna said sipping her coffee, "Me too."

Mary said, "Well, now that we are Alpha Phi we have more than kimchi story to share."

"I have a plan, said Linda." "You guys must celebrate chusok. Let's go to Flushing Meadow Park in New York for the chusok celebration dressed in Korean costume."

Jenna said, "Nobody shows up in Hanbok unless they are entertainers during the celebration there. Besides I don't want to miss school. We can go to New York some other time."

Mary interjected, "Chusok is a Korean family celebration. I don't want to do anything different on campus during a Korean holiday."

"OK, but we'll definitely wear hanbok together and have someone take photo of us three."

"I don't have any hanbok. Where can I get one?" asked Jenna.

Linda said knowingly, "I would not look in Korea town in America. I would travel to Korea and get them. You can get it everywhere at an open market, or any local hanbok maker or visit Yi Young Hee designer in Seoul. My parents got their hanbok tailor designed from Yi Young Hee, but you have to make an appointment months in advance just for measurements."

Jenna exclaimed, "I want to go to Korea."

As they were finishing their dessert they promised each other they would keep in touch during and after college.

A year later Mary, Jenna and Linda packed their hanbok and drove to Lancaster County in Pennsylvania. They found an open hilly field with a small white church in the background.

"This is a perfect spot for the photo opportunity," exclaimed Mary.

They went to a local shop and pretended to shop for things and then asked for ladies room. Then they changed to hanbok. Then Jenna asked a passerby to take a photo of them.

"Where are you from?" asked the passerby.

"We are U Penn students. We wanted to visit Amish farm. We come from South Korea."

"Is that the good part?" asked the passerby.

Linda said, "No, it's the democratic part. North is a communist country."

Passerby said, "Of course."

And he clicked away.

After the three girls had a tour of Amish farm they drove aimlessly, hoping to end up in Philadelphia. They spotted a chain drug store and a diner by the road. They decided to have an early supper at a diner. Jenna then dropped off the roll of film at the drug store's one-hour photo shop.

"We have one hour for supper then we get to see a photo of ourselves in hanbok!" exclaimed Jenna.

Girls became rowdy at a diner and had a heated debate about every professor they liked and disliked.

At the end Linda summed up, "Whatever we said about our professors here will not be uttered again."

Jenna offered, "My lips are sealed."

Mary said grudgingly, "OK. I won't talk about it."

Jenna said, brightly looking at her watch, "I'm going to pick up the photos."

The other two girls remained in the diner chatting about this and that. Three minutes later Jenna returned with an envelope with photos. Each feasted her eyes to the Korean hanbok and carefully scrutinized their facial expressions.

Mary exclaimed, "We look alike. I'm not just saying that because we are all Koreans."

"We look Chinese," Jenna said.

"No, we look Japanese," said Linda.

"No. You don't understand. We share common features. We must share kinship. I think we are related," said Mary.

Then they each shared personal history. Mary, Jenna and Linda were all born in the same year. Mary was born in March, Jenna in August and Linda in October. Mary's parents are from Pyongyang, North Korea. Her father like his father is a medical doctor. They are Northern refugees who come from well to do propertied class in North Korea, who escaped to South Korea and thereafter immigrated to the United States. Mary was born in the United States in Baltimore, Maryland. Jenna comes from Seoul. She came to America when she was five. She father owns a drug store. He is a pharmacist. The family lives in Brooklyn, so she practically considers herself a New Yorker. Her parents come from Kyungsang Bukdo

Taegu. Her grandfather had owned an apple farm there. They moved to Seoul and then thereafter immigrated to America. Both of Linda's parents come from Seoul. They had lived in Seoul for generations. Her mother is related to the next to the last King of Yi Dynasty. So her mother comes from an aristocrat among Yang ban aristocrats lineage. Linda came to America when she was thirteen with her family.

Linda had been secretive about her father's occupation. The reason is that he is an engineer and has worked for a couple of chemical companies from both of which he was laid off as a result of merger and acquisition and leverage buy out. He was jobless for a while and then the family opened up an Oriental food mart. At first his inventory consisted of perishable items such as kimchi, tofu, bean paste, ramyun etc. but later he added such things as chinaware and furniture.

After a weekly meeting during dinner at Alpha Phi house after much prodding from Jenna, Linda commented that corporate America is not the place for job security. Then she added that his father's store inventory included Korean bone china and traditional Korean furniture.

Mary asked "Who would buy Korean bone china? They are not well known, are they? I've heard of English bone china."

Linda said, "They are selling. You're right. WASPs generally would not consider buying them. But Jews would buy them."

Jenna interjected, "Korean bone china patterns are not as refined or aesthetically pleasing as Royalton or Wedgwood."

Mary said, "We don't use bona china at our home. Are they really made of bones?"

Jenna added, "Animal bone ashes."

Mary said, "They sound spooky. Like Hockus Pockus <u>I Dream of Jeannie</u> episodes."

Linda says adamantly, "Jeannies don't dwell in bone china vases. That's a fiction. An imagination."

During one lunch while Linda was eating alone, Mary joined the table.

"Remember the time we drove to Amish town and we talked about our teachers?" asked Mary with a tilt in her voice.

Linda said, "We promised we would not talk about it again."

"Well, we have a trouble at our hand. Jenna just got a job working as a lab assistant for Professor Smith."

Linda said "Uh uh. He was the reason I changed my major."

"You should talk to Jenna. We should talk to Jenna," urged Mary.

Linda made a grimace and nodded.

The next day Mary, Linda and Jenna met at a local pizzeria. Mary and Linda were waiting for Jenna to talk about Professor Smith.

Jenna began to sigh with pleasure and then said, "Professor Smith is so cute."

Jenna was lost in reverie momentarily.

Mary said coldly, "I passed by his office the other day and he was on the phone ranting about teaching an uppity yellow a lesson. Something about turning a kori into a guinea pig for his private scientific experiment. So you should stay away from him"

Linda said, "Are you the only Asian in his lab?"

Jenna nodded incredulously.

"Well then he must be talking about you."

Linda became animated and said, "I had him for intro Bio and visited him during his office hours a few time so I know him very well. Basically, just between us he is autistic and he thinks Miss Saigon is a lab procedure. You can very well end up with Manic Depression."

Jenna quipped, "If I am Miss Saigon then you must have been Madame Butterfly."

Linda said, "Which is why I changed my major from Biology to Linguistics."

Jenna interjected, "You changed your major because everyone knows you were a closet pre-med who couldn't hack the work."

Linda adds, "There are many reasons why one cannot get the grade one deserves, like sexual quid pro quo with "Miss slut-ski." I would avoid Professor Smith."

Mary added, "Professor Smith likes to go on safari trips. He can't say no to black girls, I heard. For All I know he could have AIDS."

Jenna said, "For your information African girls' politics is not what I aspire to emulate."

"Jenna, get another job," both said in unison.

Jenna was silent for a moment.

Jenna finally said "OK. I'll find a job in a library or something."

The following week Jenna was in a cafeteria wearing Alpha Phi lavaliere. She was enjoying tossed salad and diet Coke. Then Karen approached Jenna's table and started a conversation.

Karen had an angelic face with a diabolical smile. She had fine gold spun hair in a bob and sparkling blue eyes.

She noticed Jenna's lavaliere then asked, "What do you think about Millie Cooper?"

Jenna only knew Millie Cooper as one of the sexiest girls in her dorm.

Jenna said, "She resembles Beyonce Knowles."

Karen said, "Millie is not black."

Jenna said, "I'm sorry. I wasn't referring to her race. I meant just the feeling one gets when one looks at her."

Karen then nudged, "I heard that Millie Cooper comes from a bastard line of Franklin Delano Roosevelt."

"A bastard line? Is that recognized?" inquired Jenna.

Karen grinned as if she got Jenna exactly in a position where she wanted.

Karen starts to shout, "So now you look down at Millie Cooper. The first thing that comes out of your mouth is that Millie is a nigger and the next thing she is invisible."

Jenna looked puzzled, "No, I didn't say that."

At that point Karen threw her macaroni and cheese platter to Jenna aimed at her chest. Jenna was speechless.

Karen then shouted, "You are not even a bastard; you little Ching Chang Chong. Why don't you go back to where you come from!"

Then a passerby, actually a classmate of Jenna dumped turkey sandwich on Karen's silken hair.

The classmate then signaled Jenna, "Let's get out of here before this food fight escalates into World War III."

Jenna obediently followed the classmate.

Jenna said to her classmate, "I'm Jenna Hong. That kind of thing does not usually happen. You are really funny in a heroic way."

"Hi. I'm Les Hansen. You seem to be in good spirit. How about if I buy you a new sweater at the campus store?" offered Les.

Jenna said, "Thank you but no. I only live one block away."

Les said "Well then I must ask you out for a drink." Jenna responded brightly, "I'd like that."

Jenna is back in her sorority house watching TV waiting for dinner when Anna called her name.

"Your order of Alpha Phi sweat pants arrived. Come on up to my room," said Anna.

Jenna went upstairs, tried on the sweat pants and paid Anna.

"Let's go for a swim this evening," suggested Anna.

"I really have to catch up on my studies," said Jenna to try to back out.

"You're wrong. You come with me and I promise that your test scores in pre-med course will soar."

"Really? OK," said Jenna obediently.

After swimming for a half hour, they rested briefly in a sauna room then headed towards girls' locker room.

Anna changed quickly. "What are you staring at?" retorted Jenna.

Anna folded her arms then demanded, "Hurry up."

Jenna hastened and asked, "Now what?"

Anna walked toward the back of the locker room and began swerving a couple of combination locks.

"Anna, are you out of your mind? You're picking locks! We can go to jail," said Jenna in a hushed tone.

"I got it opened. It worked!" exclaimed Anna.

When she opened the locker they saw a small box filled old test papers. Jenna thumbed through them. They were

Organic Chemistry and Physics exam papers all graded
A's and A+'s by a guy named James T. Kim.

"Who is James Kim?" asked Jenna.

Anna said excitedly, "No questions asked. James T. Kim
went to Harvard Med School. That's all I know."

"OK," said Jenna and gulped.

"We have to make copies of these quickly and return
them in this very spot by tomorrow night."

"Who told you about this?"

"A Phi Delt guy told me the combination to this lock.
Look on the bright side. This is better than going over to
their house to pick up the box."

"OK, I'll make copies and you return the box back
here."

Anna said, "OK."

The following month, there was a mixer with Phi Delt.
Jenna and Linda couldn't make it as Jenna and Linda
were studying for exams. There Mary met Jake Sasaki.
Mary could not take her eyes off Jake Sasaki. Jake came
over Mary with a glass of white wine. Jake was drinking
sparkling water.

"Thank you. I'm Mary Yoon."

"Hi. I'm Jake Sasaki."

"How come you are not drinking?" inquired Mary.

"I'm the token temperate member in this house. That's why the house still stands on campus."

"What," Mary was taken aback. "Just kidding," said Jake as he touched Mary's elbow. "Are you Japanese? I'm Korean," inquired Mary.

Jake takes a sip and then said, "Yes. But actually my mother is German. She met my father while working in Tokyo some twenty something years ago."

"Did you hear about Jenna Hong and her food fight?"

"What? What food fight?" asked Mary.

"With Karen Baker. Look. I know your loyalty is with Jenna but I happen to know Karen. Karen said they were blabbing about Millie Cooper. Karen deactivated from Kappa amidst 'watermelon joke' rumor surrounding Millie Cooper."

Mary started to redden and began to cry. Then she stormed out of the House.

"Hey, wait," Jake followed hurriedly. Mary sitting outside the porch sobbing, when Jake came over and began caressing her hair.

"I didn't mean to hurt you, babe," said Jake.

"My parents are from North Korea so something like watermelon joke is a very touchy subject for me."

"Huh? I don't follow," asked Jake.

"I talked too much. Please ignore me," said Mary.

"I will not ignore you. You are not at fault," said Jake.

Jake then added, "In fact, may I see you again?"

Mary brightened and looked dotingly at Jake and nodded.

One evening Linda was studying John S. Mill's <u>On Liberty</u> when a tall Asian guy walked up to her and asked, "Do you like what you're reading."

Linda winked at him and said, "The part about tyranny of majority is interesting. Hi, I'm Linda Lee"

Asian guy asked, "Are you Korean? I'm Dave Kwon. There is a bulgoki dinner for Korean students this Friday at my apartment. Do you want to come?"

Linda asked, "Is that an invitation to me?"

"Yes," said Dave.

Linda said shyly, "Sure."

Friday came and Linda shows up in a Talbots put together outfit from head to toe. There were about fifteen students in the apartment, some hanging around in kitchen while others were sitting in the dining room and living room.

Dave Kwon said heartily, "Welcome. Glad you could come."

Linda sat next to two Korean American students all dressed in tight black top and pants ensemble looking sleek and slim.

"How come we don't see you at Korean Student Association ("KSA") meetings?" asked one Korean girl, who introduced herself as Jinha.

"Well, between my studies, piano lessons and my sorority I've been busy."

"Which house?" asked another girl.

"Alpha Phi," responded Linda.

"Is that a nice house? Are the girls nice?" The other girl asked.

Linda nodded.

Then they talked about their course works, tests and career aspirations.

Linda asked, "Do you know Dave Kwon well?"

Jinha responded, "I used to date him. I broke up with him last year. Frankly, he is a geek."

"Oh. He seems nice," murmured Linda.

Lind then gestured, "I better be going."

The President of KSA then approached Linda and said. "Whenever you're fed up with everything, or people get you down just come to our next meeting."

Linda thanked profusely then went over to Dave Kwon to say bye. Dave suggested, "Let's go for cheese steak and a beer next time. I'll call you."

Linda blushed and said coyly, "OK."

As soon as Linda walked out a girl in black shouted at the KSA President, "Why did you pose as the Pope and rendered a Prodigal son parable scene to Linda?"

The President of KSA said defensively looking puzzled, "Why she is a nice Korean girl. Everyone is welcome here. We all eat bulgoki."

The other girl in black, Jinha, interjected, "You don't know her type. She is a sell out."

Dave Kwon went up to Jinha who just uttered these words and pinched her cheek. "Ouch. That hurts," shouted the girl.

The KSA President gestured goodbye and walked out. The crowd then swiftly followed the President and soon the party was over.

The following Saturday night Linda and Dave went down to Center City and had cheese steak for dinner then Dave suggested that they drive around. They drove and drove and ended up in a shady bar in a shantytown. They were sitting by the bar and ordered bartender two beers. Dave excused himself to go to the men's room. While Linda was sipping her beer a stout man with polyester suit and gold chain accosted Linda. Linda was wearing flat boots made of mink and tan colored suede jacket and matching suede pants with black satin blouse.

"Hey, Miss Susie Wong, how about it you and me for one hour. You'd feel more comfortable off those furry boots and into my satin sheets in my bed."

Linda was flabbergasted. The stout man grabbed Linda's arm and Linda tried to escape his control. That's when Dave appeared. Dave swiftly punched the guy on his nose. The guy retaliated and pushed him to a table. Dave then got up grabbed a chair and threw at the stout man. The stout man was knocked out completely.

"Let's get out of here," said Linda and they ran out.

They quickly got inside the car and sped away. Next thing they knew they heard a couple of gunshots. One of the shots shattered the rear window.

Linda screamed.

Dave said, "Don't worry about it. They are not following us. We better not go back there. We made our presence known, sort to speak."

As they were miles away, Linda said, "I don't want anyone to know about this incident. Let's keep this a secret."

Dave said teasingly, "It will be our secret as long as you stay with me."

Linda said, "That's not a terribly difficult thing to do."

And they laughed their way back.

On Monday morning at the cafeteria as Mary was eating a bagel, Linda joined with a bowl of oatmeal. Linda was sipping her coffee when Mary asked, "How was your date with Dave Kwon."

"It was fun. I'm seeing him again," said Linda. Then asked Linda, "How was the diversity awareness workshop?"

"It was good overall. A lot of common sense. But I realize now many people do not possess that or use their senses for bad reasons for things to do. I remember in one meeting guys were saying how black brothers are killing one another and Asians are non-drivers."

"Really? Did you get a sense that the workshop was anti-white?"

"No. But they say, it's suppose to help people cope and counsel others."

"Sounds good," said Linda.

Following junior year during summer Linda invited Mary and Linda to Miami. Following their arrival in the airport in Miami Linda drove them to Mandarin Oriental Hotel.

"Wow, this is simply splendid," said Jenna.

"What a spectacular view of the water," said Mary.

"Sorry, I couldn't invite you over to my home. But painters are there and it's going to take days to paint the house. They are so snail pace."

After having a very late dinner at the hotel, Linda said good-bye, while Mary and Jenna went back to their room.

"Didn't you think the dinner's cost was heart-throbbing?"

Mary nodded and made a face.

"Let's go down stairs and see how much it costs to stay here."

After checking with the front desk they decided to leave the next day and booked a room at Hampton.

"This is one of those Linda's arrangements that people don't talk about."

Then they started to giggle.

The next few days they spent their lazy afternoons sitting by the beach in South Beach.

"No wonder you always have such a glowing tan, Linda," complimented Mary.

Linda said, "Well I must confess, when my tan is fading I apply tanning lotion. Estee Lauder."

"Do you meet guys here, Linda?" asked Jenna.

"When I'm alone I have a better luck. Yeh well. I invited one guy over to one of our semi-formals. He was going to University of Miami. Guys booed and jeered at him and not only that in the end he met up with Ellie."

"Are you mad? Jealous maybe? It sounds like Tennessee Waltz lyrics. You know about girlfriend taking away your sweetheart," prodded Jenna.

Linda said, "Not really. I barely knew him. Besides, I met another guy. He started out as my library friend. But he has evolved into someone special. He is Korean. His name is Dave Kwon."

Jenna listened intently while Mary made a face.

"You don't know what those Korean girls are saying about you and Dave," said Mary.

Mary then continued, "Apparently, his car was sent to a body shop after a wreck and when his mother found about it she hit the roof because Dave had always been a good boy. The girls were saying that his parents are terribly upset that his mother said that her son met up with a bad girl and no one knows which direction he is heading."

"Who told you that?" asked Linda.

"One of the KSA girls, Jinha, you know those bopsy twin who always like to dress in sleek black. They said they saw you at the bulgoki dinner at Dave's apartment."

Linda was flustered and the gathered her words, "I admit. Dave has been a good influence on me. We study at the library all the time. Just because he influenced me in a positive way it does not mean than I'm a bad influence on him. May be Jinha squealed on Dave's mother."

"I doubt it. That would make Jinha look even worse than she feels after she broke up with Dave."

"You know come to think of it, Dave never mentioned his parents to me. Not that I was waiting," said Linda.

"But still," said Jenna.

"Well girls, this evening my parents will be treating you at an Italian restaurant."

"OK. We better head back to the hotel. It's already approaching 5:00 PM."

"OK," said Jenna and Lind in unison.

They got up, and shook off sand.

In her senior year during Winter break Jenna invited Mary and Linda to her home in Brooklyn. Jenna lived in a two-story town house. Jenna's mother treated them to home cooked Korean meals and her father drove them around Manhattan. They went to see <u>Phantom of Opera and Sweet Charity</u>. They dined at Balthazar in Soho and Jing Fong in Chinatown.

At each restaurant, they talked about the Broadway show they saw each day.

Jenna said, "It's sad but true. When ugly things start to happen to you whether schemed by ugly people or not you start to feel ugly and become ugly and the whole world looks ugly and before you know your mind is filled with ugly things."

Mary said "I loved <u>Phantom of Opera</u>. The scenes, the props, the costumes, the songs, the cast. It was wonderful."

Linda nibbling on her food, "How come they don't serve frog's leg here at Balthazar?"

Jenna looked away and then said, "I don't know. They serve frog's leg at a French restaurant like La Grenouille in Midtown. Maybe you can all treat us there once you become a big time lawyer in New York."

"What neighborhood is this?" asked Linda looking around Balthazar and admiring at mirrors on the walls.

"This is Soho, where there are a lot of art galleries. Next time we'll go to Chinatown and go to Jing Fong above Police station."

"I want to have dim sum," said Mary peevishly.

"There are plenty of places for dim sum in Chinatown."

"Sounds good," said Linda.

The following day after watching <u>Sweet Charity</u>, they were in Chinatown.

As Linda was pouring tea, Mary was enjoying roasted Peking duck wrapped by waitress serving their table.

"You know what they say about duck. That if a woman should eat duck during her pregnancy, her baby would come out looking deformed," said Jenna.

"That's ridiculous. Chinese celebrate every New Year with roasted duck. It's like Koreans having dduk gook on the same day," said Linda.

"It sounds superstitious. But it's true. My father says the same thing about duck."

"Well then, it must be true. You're father is a physician."

"I would not want to live a life of <u>Sweet Charity</u>," said Linda.

"She dances too hard," said Mary.

"<u>Sweet Charity</u> is much more lively and the main character far more cheerful than <u>Memoirs of a Geisha</u>."

After Mary and Linda had left, Jenna's mother pulled Jenna aside and said solemnly, "We have to talk. We are sending you to an elite expensive school. Can't you befriend white girls? Why are you isolating yourself to Koreans?"

"Mom, they are my sorority sisters. They are my buddies."

"Did you see Linda's hair. She has platinum blond streaks! And how she was carrying on with your father. She is a total slut! And what about Mary. She's a typical Northern refugee. You don't what Northerners are like. We do. We fought the Koran War. They tend to cling amongst themselves. Why do you think there are churches for Northern Refugees in Seoul?"

Jenna was defiant, "Linda happens to be a sophisticated girl. She would not ruffle any feathers Mom. As for Mary, whose fault is it that there are churches exclusively for North Koreans in Seoul? Why do you think there are so many Korean churches in New York alone? I don't have to adopt your grandparents' prejudices. Quite frankly, I'm sick and tired of your Korean cronies' analogy of South Koreans being WASPs and North Koreans being Jews."

Jenna's mother was dumfounded. She fixed her hair momentarily and paused a bit.

Then finally she said, "OK. OK. You win. They are your friends."

Then she walked out of kitchen.

Weeks later Karen and another girl were eating at the cafeteria.

"Did you hear? Mary Yoon is going out with Jake Sasaki."

"You're kidding. That is so funny. I heard that Jenna Hong is dating a Norwegian rat and Linda Lee is dating a gook. They must be out of their minds if they think they can get away with everything they did on campus and pull it off by marrying off. They are going too far. Those girls are really getting under my skin. Linda the Penn whore now wants to be a lawyer and a wife. Don't make me laugh. This is a racist decision. We should do something about those queer girls to set status quo"

"Well what makes me puke is that Linda Lee made the Dean's list!"

Then the other girl inquired, "I know Linda wants to go to law school. But how do you know she is a whore."

Karen said, "Just look at the grandiose way she dresses. You can understand my position. I had to get one of my ex-boyfriends to rape her and leave cash behind her. Shit, I have a plan to kill two birds at once."

Then those two girls started whispering to each other's ear and they started to clap and giggle.

The following week Karen and her minion saw Mary Yoon enter the Psychology class. Karen's eyes popped out with rage.

Her minion couldn't figure out what was going on, and said to Karen, "Did you really tell that guy to make a harassing call to Mary and gave her signal to kill Linda Lee."

Karen said, "Yes. You know me. I'm so hot guys kill for me."

"Something is wrong," said the minion.

"What is wrong is that Mary does not speak English. She's an uppity yellow. She can't seem to work closely with white nor can she follow instruction," said Karen in an admonishing and authoritative tone.

Karen then added pensively, "I have to now come up with Plan B since Plan A failed."

The following week, the local paper featured an article about a mysterious murder of a high school prom queen named Linda Lee. Coroners are investigating the exact cause of death, the paper said.

Linda Lee was flipping out as she was reading about the death of another Linda Lee.

"Relax. She is no relation to you. She is white. She is a high school girl," said Jenna trying to calm Linda.

"But I feel shaken. So many good things have happened to me lately. I'm keeping off weight. I mean I'm staying thin. I have a boy friend and my grades are improving. Now I feel totally paranoid."

"Jenna. Do something. You are reporter for the campus paper. Do something for me at least. For my peace of mind."

Jenna thought hard. Then Jenna sighed. Jenna put her hand on her cheek trying to think of something clever.

Jenna then summed up, "Here's the situation the way I see it. If I bring it to public awareness that there was another girl in Philadelphia named Linda Lee and there is a possibility that killing rampage will continue until Linda Lee, the Korean is murdered, how are you going to feel? It's going to set a chilling tone on campus. People are going to avoid you. You are so popular on campus. You can't just broadcast that we are going to capture the real culprit. This has to be done secretively and stealthily. I mean at least from the Police point of view. Not only that we don't know all the facts. We can't jump to any conclusions. If I bring it up, it's going to heighten racial tension on campus. In all likelihood it was only one evil person that did the bad thing. We cannot treat the entire universe as criminals."

Linda listened and then said, "What you say makes perfect sense. But I have a hunch. A sort of sixth sense about it. OK, maybe I'm acting paranoid."

At that point Mary enters the scene. "What happened. Both of you look perturbed."

"We are going over the newspaper article about the death of Linda Lee, the high school prom queen. I told Linda the incident is not related to her," said Jenna.

"Oh my God. You must be shaken, Linda. Do you want to talk about it with my father? Maybe he can prescribe a medication for you during this trying time."

Linda said, "Maybe I should see a campus therapist. I don't feel good."

"That's up to you," said Jenna.

"Let's just keep a low profile for the rest of the semester. We'll be out of here soon. I don't expect to stay in Philadelphia after graduation, " said Mary.

Linda then asked Mary, "By the way, how was the diversity awareness workshop?"

"Didn't we have this conversation before? You asked me whether the workshop was anti-white?"

"Ok. Sounds good. So I'm freaking out here," said Linda.

Two months later Jenna, Mary and Linda were having lunch together.

Mary asked, "So what are you guys plan after graduation?"

Jenna said, "I'm hanging around in Philadelphia until Les finishes med school. He asked me to be with him. He got into U Penn Med School."

Mary then said confidently, "I'm engaged to Jake Sasaki. He proposed to me last Saturday night."

Jenna and Linda said in unison holding their hands, "Congratulations, we have to have candle light ceremony at the house!"

Mary nodded.

"What's your plan, Linda?" asked Mary.

Linda said, "I'm not sure. I got an offer to work as a paralegal at a very large New York firm. I'll have to see if law is suitable for me. I'm taking medication so I cannot make any drastic plans."

"What kind of medication?" asked Mary.

"The kind where if I were to sire a baby the baby might come out with six fingers or without a hand."

"I feel sick," Jenna said.

"But that's temporary. As soon as you're off medication you're be all right. Cheer up," said Mary.

Two months later just two weeks before the graduation ceremony Jenna, Mary were sitting in the living room sofa while Linda played the piano. Linda was playing Nocturne Op. 9 No. 1 by Chopin. Mary intermittently was staring at her diamond engagement ring while Jenna was lost in reverie feeling imbibed in music.

All of sudden, Anna stormed into the room looking flushed and shouted excitedly, "Guess what girls! Millie Cooper was just apprehended for killing of Karen Baker! Karen died three hours ago."

"What!" gasped Jenna.

Mary's eyes became completely round like a scared and surprised rabbit.

Linda stopped playing the piano.

Jenna, Mary and Linda became quiet and were eager to listen to Anna.

"Here is what I heard. Apparently Karen did some atrocious things to Millie and Millie did nothing. Then Millie's brother died in a mysterious car crash. Millie thinks Karen did it. Millie thinks that Karen was afraid that Millie's brother would take retaliatory measures against Karen so Karen got rid of Millie's brother. And now the rest is history."

Mary, Jenna and Linda didn't know what to make of the story. Linda quickly turned on the TV. And there was Millie hand cuffed.

Jenna said, "Oh my God."

"Look at Millie. She doesn't look a bit remorseful."

They were all glued to the TV for an hour.

"I'm speechless," said Jenna.

"Do you know Karen Baker," asked Mary looking sympathetically at Jenna.

Jenna said, "Not very well."

Linda said, "She was trying to get Ellie to join Kappa before Ellie joined Alpha Phi."

Jenna said, "What's going to happen to her entourage? Are they going to build a shrine for Karen or are they going to disband and pretend not to know Karen?"

Anna looked away. Linda got up and said, "I have to run out for my weekly piano lesson." Honest to God. People can date, party and marry whoever they want or choose not to. Karen need not be an equal opportunity lover to trespassers. God rest her soul.

Mary said, "Let's drive out to King of Prussia and go shopping. I believe an occasion like this warrants shopping therapy."

Jenna said, "I'll join you. But I have to brush my teeth first."

Anna said, "Sounds cool. I'll wait here."

Four years later after Mary is happily married to Jake Sasaki with a son while Linda Lee is married to Dave Kwon. Both Linda and Dave are lawyers. Jenna is engaged to be married to Les Hanson. They pass by a psychic and Linda suggests that they go see a psychic for fun. Jenna is hesitant while Mary seems agreeable. A moment later Jenna agrees.

They enter a small room filled with smell of sage wood incense. The walls and draperies are in scarlet and violet with gold trimmings. The woman in gypsy garb with a big mole on her face introduces herself as Sylvia. She says she is a psychic and a clairvoyant. Linda asks what the future holds for the three women.

"Wait, I feel a warm vibration. I feel a tug. Your mother is here."

"How?" asks Linda. Both Jenna and Mary looked bewildered.

The psychic tells them after looking into a crystal ball that the three women are actually clone sisters. While their legal mothers gave birth to them at different times and different places in the same year they were clones of a famous Korean pianist who was about to be married to a Norwegian lawyer working at a Boston firm. On the night that they were on their way back home from a romantic candle light dinner during which he proposed to her they were involved in a devastating car accident. He died instantaneously while she was paralyzed, severely disfigured. She remained in a hospital for weeks but she became too weak and then died.

The three girls began to sob uncontrollably. They were sobbing for nearly a half hour. Each paused a bit and thought of something to say but remained taciturn. They were speechless. When Sylvia finally demanded money, they quickly left. After that they bade each other goodbye they promised each other they would keep in touch.

By the Lake
By Dorothy Hong
(Fiction)

At about 6 o'clock in the morning a camp counselor decided to take a swim in the lake while other campers were still asleep. It was a hot August morning and already the temperature reached in the low 80's and the water seemed lukewarm. As the camp counselor continued to swim in a steady but leisurely pace and as he was kicking his right foot he felt something in his foot what felt like a fabric. So he plunged into the water and much to his horror he found remain of a dead boy, apparently someone who drowned earlier. The camp counselor dragged the dead body on to the dry land and administered first aid to no avail and so he used his cell phone to get help.

A physician examined the boy and pronounced him dead. For obvious reason the demise of the little boy was not announced at the breakfast table but the counselors

were asked about the whereabouts of the missing boy. Actually everybody knew the boy because he was the preacher's kid. The dead boy's father sponsored this special sleep away summer camp for Korean American youth in an Upstate campsite. Campers were stunned as the rumor spread right before lunch during free time as they were playing ping pong while others watched ping pong players waiting for their turn to play. There was tension and fear and kids knew soon thereafter there will have been finger pointing. In the campers' minds, this incident was all about finding out what naughty things were you doing last night, who were your friends that got you into trouble and who knew what kind of situation.

There were about thirty five campers and so the administration deemed it was worthwhile to conduct an onsite interrogation. Everybody said after the campfire gather around and sing along time they returned to their bunk bed suite. A couple of girls admitted that they continued to gather around a male camper who played the guitar in the porch but other than that they did not notice anything unusual.

Then it became evident of unspoken resentment surrounding the dead boy because he was the 'Preacher's Kid' to the extent an integral role a Korean community church played in this relatively recent immigrant group in New York area. He was dark skinned, had slightly curly hair and thick lipped. He was well dressed and was not shy of flaunting his new American wealth and the family membership to their suburban neighborhood's country club. Certain kids snickered behind his back because really kids felt they were better than the preacher's kid and more importantly they were all jealous of him and thought he was undeserving.

The purpose of a camp of this sort was for Korean youngsters to enjoy Christian fellowship and at the same time glorify God, develop a sense of positive identity of being Korean and make a realistic self-assessment about one's ability vis-a-vis one's belonging in a racial minority group and recent immigrant group in America. Some came to improve English while others came to develop friendship. Still the rest came at the urging of their parents who felt kids were developing self hate and possibly engaging in anti-social behaviors in the course of their children's relentless effort to integrate and befriend neighborhood white kids.

Each camper was given an opportunity to shed light on the mysterious death of minister's son. After some discussion among camp counselors and a social worker, they deemed another round of individual interview was warranted with some but not all campers. The following synopses were submitted for further investigation.

Camper 1: "James, the minister's son, was my friend as my father was an elder in the same church and so we had frequent contacts. I think the black dishwasher in the cafeteria did it. James was ambivalent about his sexual orientation but was reluctant to come out. He relayed to me recently the incident with black dishwasher at campsite whom he confessed had an intimate relationship over the course of years that he participated in the summer camps. I think the black guy made him pull down his pants. James said he gave away his Seiko watch but I think in reality the black guy stole it. I believe the black dishwasher was sexually frustrated and felt outraged that he was not invited in any of the Korean camp functions and/or parties."

Camper 2: "Seriously, James' family originally comes from a modest means in Korea and his father barely earned college education in a small college that no one has heard of in Korea and basically they were low born. I mean any Korean will tell you that only a dork would enter a life of ministry. But I took it in good stride that America is steeped in Puritanical tradition and that after all Harvard College was founded initially for training of ministers. Well, anyway he did not fit in with any of the cliques here at the camp and he was delusional into thinking that 'Preacher's Kid' was some sort of venerable title. It would not occur to me to harm James but I bet other kid would and possibly kill him."

Camper 3: "I believe James killed himself after the party fiasco. He wanted to organize a party but there were no many hurdles and honestly nobody cooperated because people could see right through him his devious scheme. He had a crush on a girl named Mary who was 2" taller than him but who had by far the best proportioned body. His roaming eyes were all over her at all times by the lake when we all went swimming. At one time crazy James went up to Mary and suggested that a small group play strip poker. I think in the end James realized he couldn't win Mary's heart and he felt as though he lost his face." I mean, James felt that other guys were unnecessarily inching their way in out of envy and to spite him and he couldn't cope and didn't want to deal.

Camper 4: "What happened was a bunch of us decided to play strip poker by the docks that night and things got a little unruly and next thing we noticed was that James disappeared. We thought he went back to his sleeping quarter. But I realize with hindsight now that he must have fallen into the lake and drowned. In all probability it was an accident."

Camper 5: "You know I bet you the 'ABK' ("American Born Korean") bully, Matt, killed him. Unlike other recent immigrants, Matt's family came to the US in 1950's and received their PhD's in America and thereafter stayed in America. I believe they live in a dime cent, cardboard type of suburb and you know how much a professor makes in comparison to a Korean minister. James was a rich kid with carefree lifestyle surrounded by many Korean friends who adored him. Matt, on the other hand, was a loner even though he was always lording over newcomers in a Korean crowd. What encouraged Matt to behave this way for so long was that no one dared to stand up to him and speak out. Matt would always finish his argument by asserting, 'I'm not a FOB; I was born here.' The palpable hostility between Matt and James and Matt's voracious need to feel superior to James in all aspects of life are really terrifying now that I ponder on this issue."

Camper 6: "I heard a rumor that James is a 'Tiggy' i.e. a half-breed. Even though he was relatively dark and had thick lips people guessed that he was half WASP ("White Anglo Saxon Protestant") and half Korean. I heard that the family was getting a special tax break through their adoption of James. One obvious reason why this theory holds is that James' parents never chastised him publicly or privately. On the side, I should add, we have no idea why James enjoys acting like some black kid in the ghetto but you know he thought his rendition of a black boy was pretty amusing. James had grand ideas about living a comfortable life even though by any American standard he was a boy from high class. James would always think of ways to steal enviable things just for the heck of it. One time he didn't even notice or rather he was not conscious that he had pilfered some small bric-a-brac from the church bazaar fair.

Camper 7: "I'm devastated by the whole thing. James was a beautiful, photogenic boy. He was also popular in school among white students. I'd like to close this chapter of my life by noting that it was a drowning accident because seriously everybody here is traumatized and guilt-ridden. To mar someone's life by dubbing as juvenile delinquent with very little evidence when James's parents are not even aggressive about finding perpetrator is ridiculous. There is really no evidence; I've asked around."

Camper 8: "I doubt that any Korean kid would even possibly entertain the idea of hurting James because he was the 'Preacher's Kid.' His father is very well respected. Everybody enjoys his sermon each Sunday. On the other hand, to suggest that any outsider did it is utterly outrageous when Korean community here is so small and vulnerable. I know more Asians who found themselves in dire circumstances after making vigorous efforts to prosecute or litigate society's wrongs. I want to forget about the whole thing."

Camper 9: "I think it's an act of some black thug coached by some big to do white establishment matron lady who probably argued with the minister's wife and lost an argument, perhaps over a parking space, who knows. Anyway I think this should be left a cold case because I heard that this kind of scenario is really an ugly fact of life in America. I don't anticipate any radical social reforms sweeping over American land sometime soon, so why make waves and rock the boat?"

Thirty years later the death of Korean preacher's son by the lake still remains unsolved mystery.

THANKSGIVING DINNER
BY DOROTHY HONG
(FICTION)

So it was with much anticipation Emily prepared her thanksgiving dinner for her family and her esteemed guest, Jinsoo. Emily, who was awaiting her American citizenship approval process looked back gleefully, the year after her family immigrated to Queens area in New York City, when one co-worker who was described as a Mayflower girl invited her to her apartment for a Thanksgiving dinner. The celebration there appeared to be a typical multi-ethnic gathering so Emily felt instantly at ease and knew that no awkward favor was extended on her behalf. Dinner consisted of buffet style feast with turkey, cranberry sauce, mashed potato, yam, string beans and corn. After this dinner experience Emily felt totally Americanized and welcomed to America as Emily had an intimate glimpse of a bona-fide Pilgrim dinner celebration.

Ever since the dinner they became good friends. She was especially nice to Emily because a couple of white guys showed interest in her although in a casual friendly way. Emily in turned took this opportunity as shopping extravaganza campaign. For Emily it was time to transform to weave into a more integrated American and leave behind her old self so that she would become a less noticeably aloof Korean girl from Pusan. Emily spent less and less time in Flushing and Han Ae Reum shopping mall and more and more time collecting American cookbooks, cooking each American recipe at her home. Emily stopped listening to Hyori Lee's music and gave away all the clothes she brought from Korea to Salvation Army. Like other Korean immigrants, Emily went to a neighborhood Korean church with enthusiasm and was confident enough about her English to strike up conversations with American born suburbanite Korean Americans. Emily no longer considered going back to Korea. She examined the mannerisms of second generations carefully, opting for herself as well more preppy attire that those Ivy Leagued young Korean Americans had seemed to feel so ease in.

At about that time, Jinsoo, another recent Korean immigrant noticed lively Emily and mistook Emily for an American born Korean. When Emily noted she had only been in America for five years he was thrilled and asked her out on a dinner date a local Korean Restaurant to have mixed meat and vegetable rice or otherwise known as bibimbop. One dinner date led to another date then they went out to see a series of movies and musical concerts. Now they were at a point where they would go grocery shopping together and run errands for one another. They practically spoke on the phone every day. Jinsoo worked at a Korean bank on Park Avenue while Emily worked at an American bank of global stature also on Park Avenue.

Knowing that Emily liked to cook Jinsoo suggested that he be invited to their family dinner once in awhile to get a taste of Emily's cooking. Emily was excited. She learned how to cook Korean meals watching her mother cook night after night. She also consulted Korean cookbooks. Jinsoo came from countryside right outside Inchon so he liked things like Korean style tripe, chitterlings and ox foot broth. One day she prepared ox tail soup. Ox tail broth took painstaking time and care to prepare but Emily didn't seem to mind and felt joyful when Jinsoo wolfed it down without his knowing how much care went into each sip of the soup. Jinsoo and Emily enjoyed a platonic yet exclusive boyfriend-girlfriend relationship for a year now. At the suggestion of Emily both enrolled in a night school to improve their English. Emily did better than Jinsoo in the classroom performance but that did not seem to bother Jinsoo. Jinsoo thought Emily was cute in her effort to learn English.

So the Thanksgiving day arrived. Emily got up early in the morning slaving away in the kitchen, baking and dicing and cleaning kitchen intermittently as she was cooking. She looked flushed and was perspiring all day long toiling away in the kitchen. Everything seemed to turn out perfectly. Emily was in love with Jinsoo and she wanted to please him immensely with her cooking. Emily was really looking forward to the dinner as she had prepared for the first time all American thanksgiving dinner fare modeled after her dinner invitation by a Mayflower girl some time ago.

Emily's menu in addition included Brussels sprouts with carrots in tangerine sauce, pumpkin soup, bread pudding, string beans with Bermuda onion, soy sauce with blue cheese topping and the usual turkey, yam, cranberry, corn and apple pie. Emily was waiting and waiting. For the first time in her life she felt a secret joy in feeling like a true bride of Jinsoo. She waited more. Jinsoo never showed up for the thanksgiving dinner. It was eight thirty in the evening; she tried to reach him at home and his cell phone to no avail. Finally, Emily's family had dinner without Jinsoo. Emily looked pensive as silent tears were streaming down her face.

At eleven thirty Emily finally reached Jinsoo. When Emily confronted him, Jinsoo sighed and then responded curtly, °Look, I never said anything when you lost your keys to your apartment and what not. I never said anything when you wanted me to go to Six Flags amusement park with you making me get up six in the morning. I never said anything when you bleached your hair. But this I have to say. I never want to see you again. Good bye." Jinsoo hung up. Emily was stunned. She was standing there feeling clueless, staring at the white wall listening listlessly to the dead dial tone.

Three Way Cubicles
by Dorothy Hong
(Fiction)

"Your teacher does not think you can be a lawyer. But I think you will make a good lawyer."

Those words kept echoing in her mind as Jane Pyo entered the office for her temporary assignment as a document reviewer. She studied hard in school and she wanted to reap benefit from her effort notwithstanding hostile environment she had to endure in school where teachers and peers alike didn't think there would be enough lawyer's work for Koreans in America but only in the context of criminal cases twisted with racial discrimination and personal injury matters relying on stereo types and other than that a few international corporate and litigation matters with Korean names. Why do they think that I can only exist in Korea Town eating bindaedduk (Korean

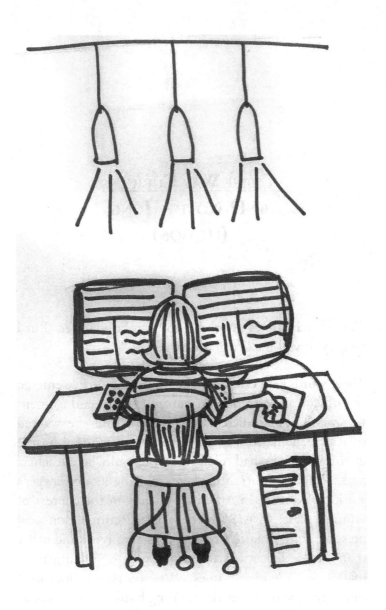

mungbean pancake) or spooning pinkleberry frozen yogurt in the urban America pondered Jane.

Having grown up letter writing to chaebol daughter from private schooling in Korea before immigrating she was then succumbed into thinking that Samsung, Hyundai and Daewoo would be her meal ticket but she knew deep inside they would rather have big blue eyes and aquiline nose European descent lawyers who can roll their tongues with greater velocity than her own with effortless ease than her measured and studied simple English as if she had some chewing to do before enunciating each word in a sentence.

"I must not fall prey to familiarity and find escapism from analogy that defies reality of who I am. I am a pioneer and I must document each day the legitimacy of my existence here for I know too well from those Johnny Come Lately upper class Korean immigrants attired in Prada and Gucci that not even fundamental rights cannot be taken for granted. Freedom entails responsibility and choice whose discernment and knowledge can only be manifested with assertion," thought Jane.

But on the other hand, she was too street smart to know that while ignorance can be bliss, no one can take away knowledge and in due course owning up to truth would empower me to resist from becoming a prey to lies and dry cleaning from having indulged in my looking through their perception.

The white lawyer showed her into a three way cubicle area with two other Korean girls both of whom were assigned to the same deal. The white girl with crisp Brooks Brothers' shirt and nondescript pencil thin gabardine skirt distributed handouts marked "attorney work product" and demonstrated the usage of forensic software.

"The responsive and nonresponsive piles..." blah blah blah.

Then she smiled, left her phone number and e-mail number on the blackboard and left the area.

"Hi, I am Jane Pyo."

The other two girls who were already there responded indifferently, "Hi, I am Grace Min."

The other girl then waved her hand and said, "Nice meeting you both. I am Sumin Kim."

Jane was dressed in polyester pattern prints from bible belt Mid-America catalogue while Grace was the epitome of L.L. Bean while Sumin exuded new wealth in what appeared to be a near perfect skin tight tailor made suit that had the smell of the high-end Fifth Avenue boutiques.

Grace asked, "Do you guys want to rotate lunch or lunch together?"

Jane Pyo said "Sure, let's lunch together."

Sumin said, "OK, me too."

They each sat down in front of their computer and with their hand on the mouse and eyes on the screen proceeded to plow through work.

Grace's watch pointed to one o'clock.

"Lunch time, girls!"

Sumin started to yawn and stretched out her arms. Jane said,

"Let's meet by the elevator. I have to run to the Ladies' Room."

Grace then said, "Let's get some gyro from the truck and sit at the public area by the stair case outside.

I don't like the smell of lamb meat because of you know what." Sumin made a small quip but decided to go along.

"It's kind of funny starting a week on Wednesday. I don't have any plans for the weekend other than cleaning and church," said Jane.

Grace then said, "I'm playing tennis this weekend. I booked the court so long ago I'm not sure at this point whether we 're still on."

Sumin then said, "Do you think our supervisor would mind if I leave early on Friday. I'm meeting bunch of people at a retreat entailing BBQ and boating."

Jane asked dutifully, "Do you know these people well?"

Sumin said, "It's all about networking. There are some cute guys so we'll see how the event unfolds."

There was certain titillation and society-lacquer-darkness about her activity that seemed totally alien to Jane's milieu. Jane has had pretty much a simple immigrant life, tight-knit Korean church life and a handful of her neighborhood friends who understood garlicky smell of kimchee because they consumed pickled tomatoes and garlic bread kind of thing. Jane remembers a time at church service during high school Christmas service she was literally pushed to sit next to a boarding school boy coming home to visit his parents both of whom were medical doctors and found herself blushing and feeling awkward and clumsy when confronted with sharing the hymnal with him. Since he showed no interest in her and at the after service social parlor he was passing around his white American cheerleader girlfriend any imagination that she could have developed in her room at home was stymied and she found herself back in community of her circle of neighborhood friends who are street smart but innocent in her assessment now that she had an experience with a carefree preppy who thought science was gauche even though that's how his parents managed to immigrate here by plane and put food on his table and send him to preparatory school.

Grace finished chewing her gyro and interjected, "Excuse me for being rude, but are these guys carrying condoms?"

Jane then teased, "Yeah, I heard about those naughty Princeton guys with baseball bat the first time."

Sumin then said spritely, "Everything is paid for. You know, it doesn't cost that much to travel if you are in good company. I used to intern for a Senator and that's how I met bunch of neat people. It's like a special group of people glued to perfection."

Jane said, "Those Senators are racists. They always make big to do with how immigrants are taking away work and complain factory work is going abroad when in fact Americans do not want to work in factories and they extended invitation to come live in USA to certain line of employment because Americans don't want to study or work in that sort of trade."

Grace squeezed Jane's shoulder and said, "Take it easy."

Sumin then said with twinkle in her eyes, "Senator is different. He is more understanding because he comes from blue collar near indigent family. Through his perspiration and pulling his own boot strap he is a self-mad millionaire and he was kind to extend this kind of his retreat trips to me. It's so exciting!"

Grace then said, "I don't know if sleeping around with Senator will help you. I'm sure as a female you can hold back. I don't know about him. But he can go home and plug his wife. And he should."

Jane scratched her head and then pondered, "How did the Senator become so rich and afford to campaign and still come out in black?"

Grace then said, "Take it easy. Just because Koreans cannot do it does not mean that other white folks can't do it."

Jane then interjected, "I'm not saying there is a simulation model for wealth creation but whoever heard of decent rich people?"

Sumin said, "Senator is totally proper and dignified. I saw him in tux once." Jane then said, "Well, you better watch your coat tail. He could just say after banging in bed. "I don't know you. I mean, what am I going to say, that you are good in bed and implicate both in immoral activity? So it's a sticky situation."

Sumin sneered at Jane and gestured to walk out, smoothing out her skirt as if to lift dirt from having sat next to Jane.

When Grace and Jane were left alone, Grace assured, "You're right. Haven't she heard of filthy rich or the obscenely rich?"

Jane then added, "Yeah, I mean where do you think those Japanese chimps learn to telephone and clean out your wallet and rice bags during the Japanese Occupation Period."

Grace said, "That's their problem that they cannot articulate crimes and injustice and have to demonstrate and act out atrocities they saw to maintain hierarchy."

Jane said, "Not every Asian can keep spirit of fun alive and refrain from regurgitating and acting out all the bad things they studied."

Grace then said, "Good thing you're a lawyer."

Jane then said, "Well, I must concede. I'm actually not into organization and order 24-7. It's so counter-intuitive and against the law of nature and gravity."

Grace then said, "You're right. At some point there will be collision vis-à-vis weight of gravity at the contact."

Jane then said, "Politicians are emotional and they make inflammatory bigoted statement for the sake of augmenting his fan number. They bully when you catch on."

Grace then said, "Don't tell Sumin that. Besides she's kinda snotty and a loner. Only God knows what she really deserves. If Koreans don't take offense to it certainly those petty white folks will."

Jane then said, "Why should I gloat when white people do away with people they don't like that coincidentally I don't like for the sake of being white when the lesson to be learned is that of racism where I am also a victim."

Grace then quipped, "You are right that we have to learn to live with and cope with people we don't like. But aren't you impressed that some people have power to inflict awful things to people who did bad things to you and get away with them because you will stay quiet after feeling satisfied?"

Jane then shook her head, "Theoretically, that's wrong and irresponsible. That's racism."

Friday rolled around. Jane and Grace were eating hamburgers from local Greek diner around the corner while Sumin was nibbling her Panini sandwich.

Jane sighed and then said after sipping her Diet Pepsi, "Life in the cubicle as a low ranking document review lawyer is neither glamorous nor appreciated. Just look at the way we are treated. No respect, no dignity. We might as well be called household slaves in the plantation South of antebellum period. Everything we earned goes to sustain our job here. We are getting crumbs while those horny law firm partners make millions."

Grace then said, "Look on the bright side. At least you get to choose your neighborhood and your clothes. It's not like hand me down uniform."

Jane then complained, "I think those white bitches speak ill about our clothes and bitch to their black lovers about putting us in our place. I don't need black condoms. I don't even like white guys as dating partners."

Sumin said, "It's not what you desire. I guess I'll be the ugly field slave today since I'll be leaving early frolicking out on field."

Grace then chimed, "Just do your timesheet right to reflect that you left early. God forbid, you don't want them to ax your body part for that. Just your pay check. Just kidding."

Jane then said, "I don't know how you can just take off. I mean from my perspective, I am now in a position to put all the ducks in a row."

Sumin said, "I can't say no to Senator."

"Grace then said, "Have fun. Send us mobile pictures through cell phone."

Sumin said, "If I have a moment."

After Sumin left the cubicle with her duffle bag, Grace tabbed Jane on the shoulder.

"Didn't she say she was going to have outdoor recreation fun as oppose to indoor? What's with the Vogue-Bazaar caliber runaway outfit?"

Sumin then said, "Shee. People might hear us. Sumin has the body for it. She is lean and willowy. Don't you think?"

Grace then said, "What's your weekend plan?"

Jane said, "I am going to do serious online job search. Korean doc review work is not worth getting burn out. These guys in the corporate governance are clueless and proud. Granted, their products are good. But I am sure there are some New York cotillion girls who are mad that their CEO daddy is not reaping benefit from their own R&D invention. Made in Korea has different nuance than Invented and created by Korean. Don't you think?"

Grace then said, "Everybody has to bite the bullet and march with time with watch synchronized with time and date of its own time zone. Otherwise they are clinically mad."

Jane then said, "For all I know they could be having leaky roof, but they are only concerned about freebees and handshake for more business."

Grace then said, "I'm kinda jealous of Sumin. I hope something bad happens to her to teacher her humility."

Jane was astounded, "You are bad. But you are allowed since you are human like me and Sumin."

Grace then said, "I didn't mean it like that. I don't want to feel the burden and be in the position to make assessment about my own perilous destiny in the event of her misfortune. It's too tiring and depressing."

Jane said, "It's more depressing if we don't know; thinking that everything's fine just because this building is made with copper and brass and marble can be harmful."

Grace said, "Seriously, when bad thoughts creep in without an ounce of evidence, that's when you know you have to leave. You know what I mean."

Jane then sighed, "I suppose. It's better to leave before fully being cognizant of all the bad things. This way it wouldn't be a lie at all for the next time if I shut my mouth about this job."

Both worked until eight in the evening and left for the weekend.

Monday arrived.

Jane showed up with a cup of coffee and donut from Arab cart pusher near the stop sign on the same block while Grace showed up well rested with a tinge of sun burn on her nose and cheeks carrying Starbucks coffee. They both arrived in the cubicle at about nine o'clock in the morning.

Nine thirty.

Ten.

Both are busily plowing through, clicking away mouse on pad cranking out responsive and nonresponsive.

Eleven o'clock and still no word from Sumin.

Noon time arrived.

Grace poked her face into Jane's cubicle area. Grace was putting her hand on her stomach.

Grace said, "I am hungry for no reason. Let's go for lunch."

"OK, I think I need a break," said Jane.

Grace who couldn't stay quiet blurted out, "Where is what's her face Sumin?"

Jane said, "She must be having too much fun. She forgot to come back."

Grace then said, "I need a sit down meal with a glass of water served."

Jane said, "Good idea. Let's go to Tempura/Sushi place that is two blocks away."

At the Japanese Restaurant they were served with warm disposable towel in a sealed plastic container. The kimono garbed waitress then brought cold glass of water and green ocha each for both. Jane proceeded to clean her hand and smoothed out what she was a fine speck of dust mingled with water droplet on the table with the used towel. Grace was breaking bamboo chopstick and playing with her set of chopsticks until she got a good grip of oshinko in a side dish.

"You don't suppose they drop the batter into sizzling hot oil on the table, do you? I see they have some concave cookery installation here."

Jane said, "I doubted it, but it would make sense for the entertainment value if the chef were to slide in live, wriggling fish into the tempura oil."

Grace interjected quickly, "How callous!"

Jane said, "I beg your pardon! That's freshness!"

Grace then gulped down some cold water and said, "Whatever. Speaking of freshness, where is Sumin again?"

Jane looked pensive then said, "I asked the supervisor and she said Sumin is not coming back. I think she quit."

Grace said, "That's a surprise. She's the one who was really after overtime and making sure she takes minimum breaks to really milk."

Jane asked, "How do you feel now that yamche (shameless) from Seoul Sumin is gone?"

Grace put her hand on her mouth as she was chewing and after she swallowed she said, "Should we be worried or move on. Does she hate us because we are so plebeian?"

Jane grimaced and said, "That's ridiculous. Even a flood survivor, a French Guillotine or Jewish Holocaust survivor needs a friend to share burden and grief."

Grace said in a matter of fact tone, "Non sequitor."

Jane said, "Sumin shows little resistance to anything other than disagreeing with our coarse and simple behavior."

Grace said, "Yeah, well she's snotty."

Jane said, "That is not to say jaded and twisted personality is reality based."

Grace then winked and said, "Do you notice how those blonde boys look so strong and formidable but yet at the same time I don't know what soft and little worn out? Maybe overwork?"

Jane picked up her tuna sushi and responded, "You never know whether they were in fact brought up on silver platter. Sumin is as well dressed as those blondies. I actually have something to show you. Sumin sent me her instant digital photo. Do you want to see it?"

Grace knitted her eyebrows and then nodded. Jane showed Grace the photo. Both remained calm and speechless to collect their thoughts.

Jane then asked, "She's turning her head and frowning. Do you suppose it is the result of thrill of ecstasy or momentary surprise sense of doom and betrayal?"

Grace then looked hard again. "If I were you I wouldn't think twice unless you want to invite danger into your own world. I say that because I care about you."

Jane then summed up, "OK. Sumin is MIA, gone. We must move on."

BLACK TO WHITE
BY DOROTHY HONG
(FICTION)

After the mysterious fire, intense investigation followed to determine whether there was a possibility of arson. Eunhae still recalls the cold frigid winter night when she came home after midnight from a disco party and was terrorized and felt immobilized at the horrific sight of big grey smoke billowing out of house and the glimpse of orangey blazing fire filling each window eager to make its way out. Her parents made their way out robed in kimono style loungewear with pajama underneath and cotton slippers. All they had in their hands were wallets and key chains.

"Where is grandpa?" asked Eunhae. Her parents looked wooden.

Then her mother spoke, "He couldn't get out of his room. We think he was paralyzed from seizure from shock."

"Do we have insurance for something like this?" asked Eunhae.

Father replied, "I'm sure. Your mother was careful in the kitchen."

Mother added, "Everything was turned off. I double checked. Maybe I forgot something that I don't remember now."

Eunhae's household was met with devastation.

Eunhae was so fear struck that she developed stomach ache, insomnia and inability to focus and people conversed with her in simple sentences in order for her to comprehend. She was also slow to pick up on things and at times seemed unaware of her surroundings.

They quickly moved to a high ceiling, post WWI apartment in a small rental apartment building a couple of blocks away from Grand Concourse in the Bronx. The tenants there were mostly senior citizens relying on social security income and others were basically recent immigrants primarily from Puerto Rico, some fair while others dark and swarthy. Their new next door neighbors were two spinster sisters who were still stubborn and spoke French notwithstanding their immigrant life in America of more than thirty years. The only thing Eunhae and those two spinsters had in common were the fact that they were all singles and preferred wearing black whenever possible.

Eunhae remembers feeling self conscious in the elevator one morning when the two sisters greeted her in their perfunctory voice "Bonjour," and getting a whiff of dense fragrance, probably made in France. Eunhae would have recognized the fragrance if they were purchased at a major department store cosmetic counter. Eunhae knows this because every weekend she dutifully shows up at Macy's on Harold Square nearby Korea Town and samples the latest perfumes, after which she goes to a local third tier Korean eatery to have spicy broth or raw fish delicacy.

Adding to misery Eunhae lost her job. Between moving and feeling distracted from exerting mental energy to find the culprit from arson, the arsonist, who brought overnight misfortune to the family Eunhae barely got by each day at work.

After three months of puttering around the cramped and damp apartment, he mother got her a job as a nanny. Basically, the job entailed cooking and cleaning, not so much babysitting since the kids were in pre-teen enrolled in junior high school. It was one of those under the table between friends kind of deal until Eunhae would find a company job.

Eunhae showed up for work in Mrs. Hahn's Scarsdale household. Eunhae diligently polished the woods, swept the floors with steamer and vacuumed the carpeted areas. She baked cakes, cookies and cup cakes for kids, distributing them with milk upon their return from school each afternoon.

"Tell me about your grandpa," asked one of the kids, eating strawberry shortcake.

Eunhae said, "He was in his nineties. Retired. Always up by six o'clock in the morning after taking his morning cold shower and insisting on having miso soup for breakfast. He alternates between reading his own publication to that of others. At other times, he just glances as magazine photos and says nothing. He taught me Chinese characters. "Hanul chun dda ji ..."

Kids inquired, "What is that?"

Eunhae responded, "They are passed down to every Korean generation for the purpose of mastery of basic Chinese characters. I think they were part of a long poem entry to the Chinese civil service examination long long time ago. The poet was then exiled as outlaw but after his demise his poetry became indispensable educational training tool for every student."

Kid then said, "A Japanese artist once said only a painter can make white into black and black into white. What do you think?"

Eunhae said, "According to Chinese poetry that I referred to once a white yarn is dyed in black as soot coloring water then the purity of whiteness can never be obtained and preserved."

Kid then asked, "What about if you use Clorox on stained clothes?"

Eunhae said, "In the textile and fabric business you usually dye in colors and patterns on white fabric not the other way around."

Kid then said, "If a kid can soil clothes with yellow stain or clothes become sallow with wear and tear then a cleaner should be able to turn yellowed fabric into white. So likewise why can't you make something black into white?"

Eunhae said, "Black is the color of mix of all primary colors. Red, yellow and blue. To make black turn white would mean to wipe out all spectrum of colors."

Kid then pointed to some grimy grayish discoloration on his socks. "Why couldn't you clean this? They are dingy."

Eunhae said, "Why don't you listen. Didn't I already tell you about the ancient Chinese poetry about a black thread never being able to return to purity of its original white color? It's very well known. Didn't your mother teach you that. It's the whole central point of East Asian pathos and aesthetics."

Kid then shouted, "My socks are dirty and it's your fault! I am going to tell Mom!"

Eunhae was stunned and then said quietly in a measured tone, "Have your mother buy you a pair of brand new white socks!"

Kid then stormed, "No! I want my white socks back!"

At this point the kid's mother walked into the house and was visibly flustered and upset that his son was screaming and shouting.

The mother hugged the child and said, "Don't worry, sweetheart."

Eunhae said, "Mrs. Hahn, I did the best I could. I put my labor of love into washing those dirty socks. That's the best that can happen in life. I don't have money so if this is important please deduct the amount of replacement white socks from my wage."

Mrs. Hahn while smoothing out his son's straight black hair said authoritatively, "That wont' be necessary. I don't mean to leave you out on the street. But clearly you cannot work here as a baby sitter. Look at my son! You have disrupted the entire household and disturbed my child. Please leave."

Eunhae walked out quickly.

She then headed to Macy's Department store even though it was not Saturday and headed to the HR department to fill out her application. After a half hour wait, she was afforded an interview.

The interviewer said, "Can you organize racks of clothes people left behind in fitting rooms and fold sweaters that people leave them out of shape?"

Eunhae said, "Yes."

Interview said, "You got the job."

Eunhae felt as though she got a new lease in life after an abrupt termination notice from Mrs. Hahn. Macy's Department store was a relatively easy commute from the Bronx. Eunhae then smiled because to her this was a promotion and in an unwitting way she used the Hahn household. But then again they fired her. In any event, Eunhae feels as though she is afforded an opportunity to develop a new character after the arson, passing away of her grandfather and her employment termination.

She purchased some black thread and needles to mend her black jacket and smiled broadly and headed home to the small Bronx apartment.